Carol Roth

Who Will Tuck Me in Tonight?

ILLUSTRATED BY
Valeri Gorbachev

SCHOLASTIC INC.
New York Toronto London Auckland Sydney
Mexico City New Delhi Hong Kong Buenos Aires

To Mark, with love —C.R.
To my grandchildren —V.G.

ISBN 0-439-78198-1

Text copyright © 2004 by Carol Roth.
Illustrations copyright © 2004 by Valeri Gorbachev. All rights reserved.
Published by Scholastic Inc., 557 Broadway, New York, NY 10012,
by arrangement with North-South Books Inc. SCHOLASTIC and
associated logos are trademarks and/or registered trademarks of Scholastic Inc.

12 11 10 9 8 7 6 5 4 3 2 1   5 6 7 8 9 10/0

Printed in the U.S.A   40

First Scholastic printing, November 2005

THE SUN WAS SETTING on the farm, and Woolly, the little lamb, was sleepy.

But Woolly couldn't find his mother.
"Oh, who will tuck me in tonight?" he asked sadly.

"I will, I will," said Mrs. Cow.
"Don't you worry, I know how.
Everything will be all right.
I'll tuck you in real snug and tight."

Then Mrs. Cow spread out the blanket and
tucked Woolly in so tight that he couldn't move.

"*Stop!*" cried Woolly. "That's not right!
Oh, who will tuck me in tonight?"

"Fancy that," said Mrs. Cat,
"I can do it, just like that!
I think I know just what you're missing.
You need lots of bedtime kissing."

Then Mrs. Cat began to lick Woolly all over
his face with her little tongue.

"*Yuck!*" cried Woolly. "That's not right!
Oh, who will tuck me in tonight?"

"Here I come," said Mrs. Horse.
"I can do the job, of course.
When you're in bed all nice and snug,
I'll give you a great big hug."

Then Mrs. Horse sat down on Woolly's bed, wrapped herself around him, and squeezed with all her might.

"*Help!*" cried Woolly. "That's not right! Oh, who will tuck me in tonight?"

"No job's too small, no job's too big!
I can do it," said Mrs. Pig.
"Don't you move, I'll be right back.
I think you need a bedtime snack."

Then Mrs. Pig brought Woolly a pail full
of messy, stinky piggy snacks.

"*No, no!*" cried Woolly. "That's not right.
Oh, who will tuck me in tonight?"

"Don't you worry, you're in luck.
I can help," said Mrs. Duck.
"Don't you fret and don't you cry.
I'll sing a lovely lullaby."

Then Mrs. Duck sang, "*Quack, quack, quack . . .
quack, quack, quack,*" but it didn't sound very
much like a lullaby to Woolly.

"*Enough!*" said Woolly. "That's not right.
Can't *anyone* tuck me in tonight?"

"I can," said Mother Sheep.

"You're back!" cried Woolly.
"Yes, my little lamb. I'm so sorry I'm late."

She tucked his blanket in just right
Not too loose and not too tight.

Gave hugs and kisses soft and sweet,
And something sensible to eat.

She sang some lovely lullabies.

Then little Woolly closed his eyes.